Rubáiyát of Omar Khayyám

Rubáiyát of Omar Khayyám

TRANSLATED BY
EDWARD FITZGERALD

WORDSWORTH CLASSICS

This edition published 1993 by
Wordsworth Editions Limited
Cumberland House, Crib Street
Ware, Hertfordshire SG12 9ET

ISBN 1 85326 187 4

Typeset by Antony Gray
Printed and bound in Great Britain by
Mackays of Chatham, Chatham, Kent

INTRODUCTION

My grandfather, born in the second half of the nineteenth century in a fishing village in the north-east of Scotland, naturally enough followed a career at sea. At one point he served as third mate on the *Persia* – an iron-built, steam-and-sail-powered packet for Cunard, which had set an Atlantic-crossing record on her maiden voyage. He got a master's ticket early, and had sailed on clippers too – jumping ship in Australia on one of his first trips, and joining the Sydney fire brigade for a year. Latterly, he sat on the bench as a police judge and JP, smoked Burma cheroots and, though he never was a regular attender himself, made sure the children were driven off to church each Sunday while he pruned his roses out in the front garden and sang snatches from 'Old Ranzo' or some other shanty. He only figures here because Omar's *Rubáiyát* was one of his favourite texts: I still have his copy, with Burne-Jones-style illustrations, and grandpa's broad-nibbed annotations and ticks of approval. He did keep the work of other poets on his shelves, but none gave much evidence of being consulted. What he found congenial in FitzGerald's translated quatrains – and what continues to provide an attraction – is one of the issues that engaged me in preparing this brief commentary on the poem and its context.

Edward FitzGerald was born in 1809, though he

didn't become a FitzGerald until 1818 when his father – with the surname Purcell – took his wife's name after she had inherited a fortune from her father. The FitzGeralds were an ancient and distinguished Irish family, though cousins had a tendency to marry (as Edward's parents did) and so the legacy of enormous wealth not uncommonly had some liabilities attached – and Edward FitzGerald blamed the obvious peculiarities of some family members on in-breeding. He himself was unconventional in many respects, but his affectionate, generous nature and droll good humour are attested to by his broad range of acquaintances and by his lively diaries and correspondence. Perhaps partly in reaction to his mother's imperiousness and ostentation, and her thwarted desire to cut a broad swathe in aristocratic and aesthetic society, the son appeared modest and unassuming, preferring a simple life in various quarters of rural Suffolk, and hating displays of wealth – though he could entertain his guests in a manner that seemed to them both lavish and whimsical.

The monotony of some aspects of rural life no doubt had an impact. On one occasion FitzGerald complained to a friend: 'Oh, if you were to hear "Where and oh where is my Soldier Laddie gone" played every three hours in a languid way by the Chimes of Woodbridge Church, wouldn't you wish to hang yourself?' – then added, 'I see, however, by a handbill in the Grocer's Shop that a Man is going to lecture on the Gorilla in a few weeks. So there is something to look forward to.' FitzGerald did have access to a broader circle of friends, including a number he had made at Cambridge and extending to close acquaintance with Thackeray, Tennyson, Carlyle and other leading figures of the time, but loneliness and a sense of separation certainly affected his disposition in particular ways, and he is a much more complex figure even than his ironic tone here would suggest.

FitzGerald's eccentricities and caprices sometimes taxed his friends, as theirs could fatigue him in turn; but both sides were willing to acknowledge compensating virtues. On one occasion, after visiting Carlyle, FitzGerald accuses himself of being 'very dull somehow, and delighted to get out into the street'. He follows this up by saying: 'Carlyle was rather amazed to see me polka down the pavement. He shut his street door – to which he always accompanied you – with a kind of groan.' But Carlyle was well aware of FitzGerald's gifts, thanking him once for a 'friendly, human' letter by saying: 'One gets so many *in*human letters, ovine, bovine, porcine, etc., etc. I wish you would write a little oftener.'

The depth of mind that lay beneath what a biographer described as the 'slightly farcical exterior' of FitzGerald was appreciated by Edward Cowell, who described him as 'a man of *real* power' – adding: 'There is something so very *solid* and *stately* about him, a kind of slumbering giant, or silent Vesuvius. It is only at times that the eruption comes, but when it *does* come, it overwhelms you!' This judgement may have been coloured by the fact that Cowell was only eighteen when they met – FitzGerald being thirty-five – but the two came to share an intellectual respect for each other, and it was Cowell who persuaded the older man to take up some readings in Persian. Cowell in fact went on to become a capable Oriental scholar, encouraged and supported by FitzGerald, although for his own part the latter described himself, fairly accurately, as a person who 'neither merits nor desires any honourable mention as a Persian Scholar, being none'. However, with Cowell's assistance he brought out a version of Háfiz's *Salámán and Absál* in 1855, and the following year was introduced to some quatrains (or *rubáiyát*) which Cowell had discovered in a manuscript in the Ouseley collection at the Bodleian Library. As FitzGerald put it in a letter to Tennyson, these were 'some curious Infidel and Epicurean Tetrastichs by a Persian of the Eleventh Century', and it was in this fashion that 'old Khayyám' first hobnobbed with his nineteenth-century transmogrifier.

FitzGerald's study of this manuscript, and another which Cowell subsequently forwarded to him from Calcutta, occupied and sustained him during the latter months of his brief and disastrous marriage to Lucy Barton, daughter of an old friend. FitzGerald had been backed into this arrangement by a mix of vagueness and misunderstanding, but found it impossible to extricate himself honourably from the ensuing marriage. This in spite of the fact that friends on either side of the match were in no doubt the parties were horribly mis-suited. Anyway, as the painful process of separation and settlement was arranged, FitzGerald elected to claim 'nine tenths of the Blame', and having first made some attempts in 'bad Latin', set about producing his version of Omar's work which provided, he said, 'a sort of Consolation'.

FitzGerald in his tetrastichs (a word from Greek prosody for a four-line set or stanza) improvised on Khayyám's originals rather than aiming for close and literal translation. He would read over sections until the gist was fixed in his mind, then go for a walk to work out his verses. Prepared to take pains, he none the less wanted 'a live sparrow' rather than 'a stuffed eagle' and insisted, 'at all Cost, a Thing must *live*: with a transfusion of one's own worst Life if one can't retain the Original's better'.

In shaping an eclogue – a pastoral poem, with an emphasis on the pleasures of beauty – and setting it in a garden, FitzGerald narrowed the scope of Khayyám's poems, and gave his own work a more obvious structure. He pointed to the pattern of a single day and of the seasons for instance, introduced an element of drama, and was influenced in his selection to some extent by limiting what might give offence to his likely audience. Although he thought of the poem as profoundly sad, that isn't the impression borne out by reading it: but it probably reflects his prevailing mood during its composition. In fact he catches something of the wit and good humour that Khayyám conjured, while omitting more directly pious verses, as well as those that were ribald or irreverent. He was always sensitive to the religious scruples of some of his closest friends (Cowell included), though his own beliefs had long since strayed beyond the fold of conventional religion, and it turned out he was very much in tune with changing tastes and attitudes at the time. J. S. Mill's *On Liberty*, Samuel Smiles's

Self-Help and Darwin's *On the Origin of Species* were all published in the same year as his *Rubáiyát*.

The views of Omar Khayyám (1048–1131) on the nature of reality deeply engaged his English translator. Khayyám was a resourceful mathematician and leading astronomer, who played an important role at one stage in reforming the Moslem calendar. Jurisprudence, history and medicine apparently engaged him too. Just what exactly was his relation to the Muslim faith and particularly the Sufic way of thought, with its emphasis on mysticism and allegory, is still a matter for lively and sometimes rancorous debate.

FitzGerald responded to what he saw as an honest and sceptical reaction to key metaphysical questions. He conceded that some stanzas required a mystical interpretation – where references to wine and intoxication became images for 'Divine Love' for example – but for him the sensual imagery did not in the first instance refer to inexpressible mysteries. The 'material Epicurean' side was what he chose to highlight: he plumped for a view of the poet as philosopher, discarding religious certainties, admitting man's frailties, accepting modest pleasures and brooding directly on the most puzzling aspects of existence. He thought Omar 'too honest of Heart as well as of Head' to be a mystic; and, setting aside the elements of divine allegory, claimed: 'his Wine is the veritable Juice of the Grape; his Tavern where it was to be had; his Sáki, the Flesh and Blood that poured it out for him; all which, and where the Roses were in Bloom, was all he profess'd to want of this World or to expect of Paradise.'

Whether he was ultimately correct in this view, that was what motivated him and drew him to his Persian counterpart. He found an echo of his own emotions and, rejecting pure spirituality – though not a kindred spirit – identified with the man himself. To the over-serious Cowell (who tended to undervalue some aspects of the poet, being too aware of the 'heathen') FitzGerald said: 'But in truth I take old Omar rather more as my property than yours: he and I are more akin, are we not? You see all [his] Beauty, but you can't feel *with* him in some respects as I do.'

Khayyám's invitations to close and amiable friendship, his urging to take pleasure in immediate joy, struck an obvious chord. Although the exotic settings of the original poems were part of their appeal, and FitzGerald if anything emphasised that exoticism, the famous setting:

Here with a Loaf of Bread beneath the Bough,
A Flask of Wine, a Book of Verse – and Thou
Beside me . . .   (verse 9)

is easily transformed to Fitz's garden of Boulge Cottage (or equivalent) where the unnamed companion is both guest and loving friend. The ironies of the poem are directed against the prescriptions and snares of conventional doctrine – FitzGerald being well aware that plenty would respond to this as 'wicked'. The pathos derives, as ever, from the death of all things lovely, and the thwarting of 'Heart's Desire' (verse 73). FitzGerald avoids nihilism by creating his corner in the midst of 'Hubbub' (verse 45), refusing to be put upon (verse 30), and even rebuking the Almighty with mischievous intent (verse 68). In quatrain 48, the approach of the Angel has something erotic in the nature of the invitation, and the implication of courage provides a balance to those stanzas where the final answer is reckoned in dust.

FitzGerald's anonymously printed booklet had an uncertain start, and narrowly escaped oblivion, being consigned to the bargain box by his publisher, and offered for a penny, reduced from a shilling. It was, however, taken up almost by chance, most importantly by Rossetti and the Pre-Raphaelite circle, together with Ruskin, Swinburne and Morris (though *not* Carlyle, who thought it a waste of time, notwithstanding his later note to FitzGerald that the poem was 'a jewel of its kind'). FitzGerald, indifferent to its success at first, being taken up with the accidental death of one of his dearest friends, William Browne, eventually prepared four editions, each one revised in many details. He saw the first pirated edition (in India) and the almost exponential expansion of a coterie of admirers, especially in America. There in due course two of the great poets of Modernism, T. S. Eliot and Ezra Pound, felt the influence of FitzGerald's version. Eliot on first reading it said 'the world appeared painted anew, in bright, delicious, and painful colours'.

Since then critical reaction has varied. There was open hostility and condescension from Robert Graves and his collaborator Omar Ali-Shah, who stressed what they claimed as Khayyám's Sufi origins, and accused FitzGerald of debasing the original to pander to defeatist and anti-devotional taste. More recently, the critic Daniel Schenkel compared Eliot's 'The Love Song of J. Alfred Prufrock' (which has an echo of FitzGerald's 'Some little Talk awhile of ME and THEE') with the *Rubáiyát*, exploring 'why we fail to respond' to the earlier poem 'as a work of serious literary art'. He nevertheless concludes: 'Perhaps now . . . Prufrock and his peers have worn thin enough to allow the strangeness of Omar Khayyám to peep through again.'

My grandfather carved the name 'Persia' with a penknife in the cover of the black-bound notebook he used as a log. For him the name of the ship, and the country, was bound up in the activities of his youth and the preoccupations of age. What did he take from the *Rubáiyát* that kept him at it? I would suggest: 'In doubt, in thrall, make the best of it; love beauty; keep an eye out for the infinite doings.' The last photograph I have of him was taken somewhere in Morocco. He is standing in a courtyard before what looks like a white marble fountain. With him is a handsome Arab, slightly younger, of equal girth, in a flowing *djellabah*, smiling broadly. My grandfather wears a sober three-piece suit, watch fob, Homburg hat (soft felt, narrow brim, dented crown). On the back of the snap – whether accurately or ironically I cannot tell – he has written: 'With the Sultan at the palace'. They appear to have their arms round each other's shoulders. Whichever casual hunter took the shot has caught them neatly in a noose of light.

ALEXANDER HUTCHISON

SELECTED BIBLIOGRAPHY

A. J. Arberry, *Omar Khayyám and FitzGerald*, London 1959

Edward FitzGerald, *A FitzGerald Medley*, ed. Charles Ganz, London 1933

Edward FitzGerald, *FitzGerald to His Friends: Selected Letters*, ed. Alethea Hayter, London 1979

Edward FitzGerald, *The Letters of Edward FitzGerald*, eds. A. McK. and A. B. Terhune, 4 vols, Princeton 1980

Edward FitzGerald, *Selected Works*, ed. Joanna Richardson, Cambridge, Massachusetts 1963

Edward FitzGerald, *The Variorum and Definitive Edition of the Poetical and Prose Writings of Edward FitzGerald*, ed. George Bentham, 7 vols, New York 1967

Robert Graves and Omar Ali-Shah, *The Rubaiyyat of Omar Khayaam: A New Translation with Critical Commentaries*, London 1967

Iran B. H. Jewett, *Edward FitzGerald*, Boston 1977

Robert Bernard Martin, *With Friends Possessed: A Life of Edward FitzGerald*, London 1985

Daniel Schenkel, 'Fugitive Articulation: An Introduction to the *Rubáiyát of Omar Khayyám*', *Victorian Poetry*, 19 (1981), 49–64

A. McK. Terhune, *The Life of Edward FitzGerald*, London 1947

I

Awake! for Morning in the Bowl of
Night

Has flung the Stone that puts the
Stars to Flight:

And Lo! the Hunter of the East
has caught

The Sultan's Turret in a Noose of
Light.[1]

2

Dreaming when Dawn's Left Hand
  was in the Sky

I heard a voice within the Tavern cry,

  'Awake, my Little ones, and fill the
  Cup

Before Life's Liquor in its Cup be
  dry.'[2]

❧ 3 ❧

And, as the Cock crew, those who
    stood before

The Tavern shouted – 'Open then
    the Door!

    You know how little while we have
        to stay,

And, once departed, may return no
    more.'

4

Now the New Year reviving old
  Desires,

The thoughtful Soul to Solitude
  retires,

  Where the WHITE HAND OF
    MOSES on the Bough

Puts out, and Jesus from the Ground
  suspires.[3]

5

Iram indeed is gone with all its Rose,

And Jamshýd's Sev'n-ring'd Cup
 where no one knows;

But still the Vine her ancient ruby
 yields,

And still a Garden by the Water
 blows.[4]

⟨6⟩

And David's Lips are lock't; but in
  divine

High piping Pehleví, with 'Wine!
  Wine! Wine!

  Red Wine!' – the Nightingale cries
    to the Rose

That yellow Cheek of her's to
  incarnadine.[5]

7

Come, fill the Cup, and in the Fire of
Spring

The Winter Garment of Repentance
fling:

The Bird of Time has but a little
way

To fly – and Lo! the Bird is on the
Wing.[6]

~~~ 8 ~~~

And look – a thousand Blossoms with
   the Day

Woke – and a thousand scatter'd into
   Clay:

And this first Summer Month that
   brings the Rose

Shall take Jamshýd and Kaikobád
away.

9

But come with old Khayyám, and
leave the Lot

Of Kaikobád and Kaikhosrú forgot:

Let Rustum lay about him as he
will,

Or Hátim Tai cry Supper – heed
them not.[7]

❧ 10 ❧

With me along some Strip of
    Herbage strown

That just divides the desert from the
    sown,

    Where name of Slave and Sultan
        scarce is known,

And pity Sultan Mahmud on his
    Throne.

II

Here with a Loaf of Bread beneath
    the Bough,

A Flask of Wine, a Book of Verse –
    and Thou

Beside me singing in the
    Wilderness –

And Wilderness is Paradise enow.[8]

12

'How sweet is mortal Sovranty!' –
   think some:

Others – 'How blest the Paradise to
   come!'

   Ah, take the Cash in hand and
      waive the Rest;

Oh, the brave Music of a *distant*
   Drum! [9]

❧ 13 ❧

Look to the Rose that blows about
us – 'Lo,

Laughing,' she says, 'into the World
I blow:

At once the silken Tassel of my
Purse

Tear, and its Treasure on the Garden
throw.'[10]

14

The Worldly Hope men set their
  Hearts upon

Turns Ashes – or it prospers; and
  anon,

  Like Snow upon the Desert's dusty
    Face

Lightning a little Hour or two – is
  gone.

15

And those who husbanded the
    Golden Grain,

And those who flung it to the Winds
    like Rain,

    Alike to no such aureate Earth are
      turn'd

As, buried once, Men want dug up
    again.

ꞏ 16 ꞏ

Think, in this batter'd Caravanserai

Whose Doorways are alternate Night
and Day,

How Sultan after Sultan with his
Pomp

Abode his Hour or two and went his
way.[11]

❧ 17 ❧

They say the Lion and the Lizard
  keep

The Courts where Jamshýd gloried
  and drank deep:

  And Bahrám, that great Hunter –
    the Wild Ass

Stamps o'er his Head, and he lies fast
  asleep.[12]

18

I sometimes think that never blows
so red

The Rose as where some buried
Cæsar bled;

That every Hyacinth the Garden
wears

Dropt in its Lap from some once
lovely Head.

19

And this delightful Herb whose
tender Green

Fledges the River's Lip on which we
lean –

Ah, lean upon it lightly! for who
knows

From what once lovely Lip it springs
unseen!

20

Ah, my Belovéd, fill the Cup that clears

Today of past Regrets and future Fears –

Tomorrow? – Why, Tomorrow I may be

Myself with Yesterday's Sev'n Thousand Years.[13]

❧ 21 ❧

Lo! some we loved, the lovliest and
  best

That Time and Fate of all their
  Vintage prest,

  Have drunk their Cup a Round or
    two before,

And one by one crept silently to
  Rest.

22

And we, that now make merry in the
Room

They left, and Summer dresses in
new Bloom,

Ourselves must we beneath the
Couch of Earth

Descend, ourselves to make a
Couch – for whom?

ᵉ≥ 23 ᵉ≥

Ah, make the most of what we yet
may spend,

Before we too into the Dust descend;

Dust into Dust, and under Dust, to
lie,

Sans Wine, sans Song, sans Singer,
and – sans End!

❧ 24 ❧

Alike for those who for TODAY
  prepare,

And those that after a TOMORROW
  stare,

  A Muezzin from the Tower of
    Darkness cries,

'Fools! your Reward is neither Here
  nor There!'

25

Why, all the Saints and Sages who
    discuss'd
Of the Two Worlds so learnedly, are
    thrust
    Like foolish Prophets forth; their
      Words to Scorn
Are scatter'd, and their Mouths are
    stopt with Dust.

26

Oh, come with old Khayyám, and
leave the Wise

To talk; one thing is certain, that Life
flies;

One thing is certain, and the Rest
is Lies;

The Flower that once has blown for
ever dies.

27

Myself when young did eagerly
frequent

Doctor and Saint, and heard great
Argument

About it and about; but evermore

Came out by the same Door as in I
went.

❧ 28 ❧

With them the Seed of Wisdom did
  I sow,

And with my own hand labour'd it to
  grow:

And this was all the Harvest that I
  reap'd –

'I came like Water and like Wind I
  go.'

29

Into this Universe, and *why* not
knowing,

Nor *whence*, like Water willy-nilly
flowing:

And out of it, as Wind along the
Waste,

I know not *whither*, willy-nilly
blowing.

30

What, without asking, hither hurried
   whence?

And, without asking, *whither* hurried
   hence!

   Another and another Cup to
      drown

The Memory of this Impertinence![14]

ॐ 31 ॐ

Up from Earth's Centre through the
    Seventh Gate

I rose, and on the Throne of Saturn
    sate,

And many Knots unravel'd by the
    Road;

But not the Knot of Human Death
    and Fate.[15]

32

There was a Door to which I found
no Key:

There was a Veil past which I could
not see:

Some little Talk awhile of ME and
THEE

There seemed – and then no more of
THEE and ME.

33

Then to the rolling Heav'n itself I
cried,

Asking, 'What Lamp had Destiny to
guide

Her little Children stumbling in
the Dark?'

And – 'A blind Understanding!'
Heav'n replied.

34

Then to this earthen Bowl did I
adjourn

My Lip the secret Well of Life to
learn:

And Lip to Lip it murmur'd –
'While you live

Drink! – for once dead you never
shall return.'

35

I think the Vessel, that with fugitive

Articulation answer'd, once did live,

And merry-make; and the cold Lip
I kiss'd

How many Kisses might it take – and
give!

❧ 36 ❧

For in the Market-place, one Dusk of
   Day,
I watch'd the Potter thumping his
   wet Clay:
And with its all obliterated Tongue
It murmur'd – 'Gently, Brother,
   gently, pray!'

37

Ah, fill the Cup – what boots it to
    repeat

How Time is slipping underneath
    our Feet:

    Unborn TOMORROW, and dead
    YESTERDAY,

Why fret about them if TODAY be
    sweet!

38

One Moment in Annihilation's
   Waste,

One Moment, of the Well of Life to
   taste –

   The Stars are setting and the
     Caravan

Starts for the Dawn of Nothing –
   Oh, make haste!

39

How long, how long, in infinite
  Pursuit

Of This and That endeavour and
  dispute?

  Better be merry with the fruitful
    Grape

Than sadden after none, or bitter,
  Fruit.

40

You know, my Friends, how long
   since in my House

For a new Marriage I did make
   Carouse:

   Divorced old barren Reason from
      my Bed,

And took the Daughter of the Vine
   to Spouse.

❧ 41 ❧

For 'Is' and 'Is-not' though *with* Rule and Line,

And Up-and-down *without* I could define,

   I yet in all I only cared to know,

Was never deep in anything but – Wine.

42

And lately, by the Tavern Door
agape,

Came stealing through the Dusk an
Angel Shape

Bearing a Vessel on his Shoulder;
and

He bid me taste of it; and 'twas – the
Grape!

43

The Grape that can with Logic
    absolute

The Two-and-Seventy jarring Sects
    confute:

    The subtle Alchemist that in a
        Trice

Life's leaden Metal into Gold
    transmute.[16]

44

The mighty Mahmud, the victorious
  Lord,

That all the misbelieving and black
  Horde

Of Fears and Sorrows that infest
  the Soul

Scatters and slays with his enchanted
  Sword.[17]

45

But leave the Wise to wrangle, and
with me

The Quarrel of the Universe let be:

And, in some corner of the
Hubbub coucht,

Make Game of that which makes as
much of Thee.

❧ 46 ❧

For in and out, above, about, below,

'Tis nothing but a Magic Shadow-
show,

Play'd in a Box whose Candle is
the Sun,

Round which we Phantom Figures
come and go.[18]

47

And if the Wine you drink, the Lip
you press,

End in the Nothing all Things end
in – Yes –

Then fancy while Thou art, Thou
art but what

Thou shalt be – Nothing – Thou
shalt not be less.

❧ 48 ❧

While the Rose blows along the
River Brink,

With old Khayyám and Ruby Vintage
drink:

And when the Angel with his
darker Draught

Draws up to Thee – take that, and do
not shrink.

49

'Tis all a Chequer-board of Nights
and Days

Where Destiny with Men for Pieces
plays:

Hither and thither moves, and
mates, and slays,

And one by one back in the Closet
lays.

50

The Ball no Question makes of Ayes
   and Noes,

But Right or Left, as strikes the
   Player goes;

And He that toss'd Thee down
   into the Field,

He knows about it all – HE knows –
   HE knows!¹⁹

51

The Moving Finger writes; and,
   having writ,

Moves on: nor all thy Piety nor Wit

   Shall lure it back to cancel half a
      Line,

Nor all thy Tears wash out a Word
   of it.

52

And that inverted Bowl we call The
  Sky,

Whereunder crawling coop't we live
  and die,

  Lift not thy hands to *It* for help –
    for It

Rolls impotently on as Thou or I.

53

With Earth's first Clay They did the
  Last Man's knead.

And then of the Last Harvest sow'd
  the Seed:

  Yea, the first Morning of Creation
    wrote

What the Last Dawn of Reckoning
  shall read.

54

I tell Thee this – When, starting
   from the Goal,

Over the shoulders of the flaming
   Foal

Of Heav'n Parwín and Mushtarí
   they flung,

In my predestin'd Plot of Dust and
   Soul.[20]

❧ 55 ❧

The Vine had struck a Fibre; which
about

If clings my Being – let the Sufi
flout;

Of my Base Metal may be filed a
Key,

That shall unlock the Door he howls
without.[21]

◌ 56 ◌

And this I know: whether the one
    True Light,

Kindle to Love, or Wrath – consume
    me quite,

    One Glimpse of It within the
        Tavern caught

Better than in the Temple lost
    outright.

57

Oh, Thou, who didst with Pitfall and
with Gin

Beset the Road I was to wander in,

Thou wilt not with Predestination
round

Enmesh me, and impute my Fall to
Sin?

58

Oh, Thou, who Man of baser Earth
  didst make,

And who with Eden didst devise the
  Snake;

  For all the Sin wherewith the Face
  of Man

Is blacken'd, Man's Forgiveness
  give – and take![22]

Kúza-Náma

❧ 59 ❧

Listen again. One Evening at the
Close

Of Ramazán, ere the better Moon
arose,

In that old Potter's Shop I stood
alone

With the clay Population round in
Rows.[23]

60

And, strange to tell, among that
   Earthen Lot

Some could articulate, while others
   not:

And suddenly one more impatient
   cried –

'Who *is* the Potter, pray, and who the
   Pot?'

61

Then said another – 'Surely not in
  vain

My Substance from the common
  Earth was ta'en,

  That He who subtly wrought me
    into Shape

Should stamp me back to common
  Earth again.'

62

Another said – 'Why, ne'er a peevish
  Boy,

Would break the Bowl from which he
  drank in Joy;

Shall He that *made* the Vessel in
  pure Love

And Fancy, in an after Rage destroy!'

63

None answer'd this; but after Silence
spake

A Vessel of a more ungainly Make:

'They sneer at me for leaning all
awry;

What! did the Hand then of the
Potter shake?'

༄ 64 ༄

Said one – 'Folks of a surly Tapster
  tell,

And daub his Visage with the Smoke
  of Hell;

  They talk of some strict Testing of
    us – Pish!

He's a Good Fellow, and 'twill all be
  well.'

❧ 65 ❧

Then said another with a long-drawn
Sigh,

'My Clay with long oblivion is gone
dry:

But, fill me with the old familiar
Juice,

Methinks I might recover by-and-
bye!'

66

So while the Vessels one by one were
  speaking,

One spied the little Crescent all were
  seeking:

  And then they jogg'd each other,
    'Brother! Brother!

Hark to the Porter's Shoulder-knot
  a-creaking!'

❧ 67 ❧

Ah, with the Grape my fading Life
    provide,

And wash my Body whence the Life
    has died,

    And in a Windingsheet of Vine-
        leaf wrapt,

So bury me by some sweet Garden-
    side.[24]

68

That ev'n my buried Ashes such a
   Snare
Of Perfume shall fling up into the
   Air,
   As not a True Believer passing by
But shall be overtaken unaware.

69

Indeed the Idols I have loved so long

Have done my Credit in Men's Eye
much wrong:

Have drown'd my Honour in a
shallow Cup,

And sold my Reputation for a Song.

70

Indeed, indeed, Repentance oft
   before

I swore – but was I sober when I
   swore?

   And then and then came Spring,
      and Rose-in-hand

My thread-bare Penitence apieces
   tore.

71

And much as Wine has play'd the
   Infidel,

And robb'd me of my Robe of
   Honour – well,

   I often wonder what the Vintners
      buy

One half so precious as the Goods
   they sell.

72

Alas, that Spring should vanish with
the Rose!

That Youth's sweet-scented
Manuscript should close!

The Nightingale that in the
Branches sang,

Ah, whence, and whither flown
again, who knows!

73

Ah Love! could thou and I with Fate conspire

To grasp this sorry Scheme of Things entire,

Would not we shatter it to bits – and then

Re-mould it nearer to the Heart's Desire!

74

Ah, Moon of my Delight who
  know'st no wane,

The Moon of Heav'n is rising once
  again:

How oft hereafter rising shall she
  look

Through this same Garden after
  me – in vain![25]

❦ 75 ❦

And when Thyself with shining Foot
   shall pass

Among the Guests Star-scatter'd on
   the Grass,

   And in thy joyous Errand reach the
     Spot

Where I made one – turn down an
   empty Glass![26]

TAMÁM SHUD

NOTES

1 The throwing of a stone into a cup or bowl was the signal for the hunt to get underway. FitzGerald changed the content of this evocative and dramatic opening quatrain in later editions – much to the regret of contemporaries like Swinburne.

2 The first line refers to a kind of false dawn – before true daybreak. Perhaps in retrospect FitzGerald described how Omar's thoughts appear to follow the pattern of one day: 'He begins with Dawn, pretty sober and contemplative, then, as he thinks and drinks, grows savage, blasphemous, etc., and then sobers down into melancholy at nightfall.'

3 FitzGerald observes that the New Year here belongs to the vernal equinox, and comments on the sudden onset of spring – with blossoms on trees and flowers appearing before the snow is well off the ground. He also refers to Jamshýd, the ruler *whose yearly calendar* [Khayyám] *had helped to rectify* (FitzGerald's note: EFG). For Moses, see Exodus iv: 6. The healing power of Jesus' breath is also alluded to.

4 *Iram* [was a garden] *planted by King Shaddád, and now sunk somewhere in the sands of Saudi Arabia. Jamshýd's Seven-ring'd Cup was typical of the seven Heavens, seven planets, seven seas, etc., and was a Divining Cup* (EFG).

5   *Pehleví, the old Heroic Sanskrit of Persia. Háfiz also speaks of the Nightingale's Pehleví which did not change with the People's* (EFG).

6   Robert Graves says this stanza is derived from a poem by Attar, *Mantiq Taiyur*, which FitzGerald had read and translated as 'Bird Parliament'.

7   *Rustum, the 'Hercules' of Persia, and Zál his father* (EFG). Hátim Tai was a philanthropist, famous for his generosity. FitzGerald's inclusion of cities and figures from Persian history was part of his aim of preserving oriental forms for poetic effect. In some respects he thought it 'better to be orientally obscure than Europeanly [*sic*] clear'.

8   Another famous stanza FitzGerald fiddled with repeatedly – without significant improvement. Graves's supposedly more accurate version is not superior:

> A gourd of red wine and a sheaf of poems –
> A bare subsistence, half a loaf, not more –
> Supplied us two alone in the wide desert:
> What Sultan could we envy on his throne?

Martin, in his biography, notes how FitzGerald deliberately obscured the gender of the beloved in his poem. 'In the original both a woman, or houri, and a youth, are addressed in the love poetry, as was the custom of Omar and his contemporaries.' FitzGerald, by contrast, he says, leaves the sex 'an open question' (p.208).

9   The second edition's 'Glories of This World' makes the sense of the first line clearer.

10   *That is, the Rose's Golden Centre* (EFG).

11 A caravanserai is an inn with a inner courtyard where travellers might rest.

12 Persepolis was called 'The Throne of Jamshýd,' and he was reputed to be its founder. Bahrám Gúr, a Sassanian king of Persia, was named after his fondness for hunting the wild ass, or onager.

13 'Sev'n Thousand Years': the supposed age of the world. *A thousand years to each planet* (EFG).

14 The 'impiety' of this and similar verses could be reckoned to give offence. Although he had given copies of other texts to his childhood friend Mary Lynn, he was aware that she would not approve the agnosticism evident in certain sections of the *Rubáiyát*. He told her: 'I shall not give you a copy of *Omar Khayyám*, you would not like it.' To which she simply replied: 'I should not like it.' 'He was very careful,' commented Miss Lynn, 'not to unsettle the religious opinions of others.'

15 *Saturn, Lord of the Seventh Heaven* (EFG).

16 *The Seventy-two religions supposed to divide the World, including Islamism, as some think: but others not* (EFG).

17 Sultan Mahmud conquered India at one point.

18 *A Magic-lantern still used in India; the cylindrical Interior being painted with various Figures, and so lightly poised and ventilated as to revolve around the lighted candle within* (EFG).

19 The game in Khayyám's original is polo.

20 *Parwín and Mushtarí – The Pleiades and Jupiter* (EFG). FitzGerald is obviously conscious of the significance of astronomy to Khayyám, just as he is aware of the concepts of logic, physics and

mathematics that are slipped into the poems. In a later annotation he describes a mathematical quatrain where Khayyám anticipates John Donne's celebrated metaphor of 'twin compasses' to describe the relationship of lovers.

21 Robert Graves complains (with some justice) that the first two lines here are 'clumsy to the point of unintelligibility'. He adds: 'The "struck Fibre of the vine" in FitzGerald's version is lifted from another Persian poet; and the inclusion of anti-Sufi propaganda seems in part due to pique against a rival translator, M. Nicolas, the French Consul at Resht.' Nevertheless, he goes on: 'Khayaam may well have privately mocked the "painted" or false Sufis, very much as Jesus denounced the "painted" Pharisees . . .' (pages 17–18). It needs to be emphasised, however, as FitzGerald acknowledged, that Sufism has inspired the works of some of Persia's finest poets, including Attar.

22 Terhune (page 219) quotes one Persian scholar who maintains that Khayyám's 'addresses to the Deity, even when most audacious, are those of a convinced believer; sometimes offering the advice of an intrepid subject to his sovereign, sometimes throwing out the shrewd comments of a court jester'. Cowell, obviously distressed by FitzGerald's riposte in this quatrain, maintained that FitzGerald 'mistook the meaning of giving and accepting in the last line out of his own mistake. I wrote to him about it when I was in Calcutta; but he never cared to alter it.' FitzGerald, not especially repentant, responded: 'As to my making Omar worse than

he is in that stanza about Forgiveness . . . it is very likely I may have construed, or remembered, erroneously. But I do not *add* dirt to Omar's face.' Terhune claimed FitzGerald himself 'was no more unorthodox, although he was more outspoken, than many of his contemporaries who acknowledged doubts while searching for faith. He then quotes FitzGerald's view that in the *Rubáiyát* he discovered 'a desperate sort of Thing, unfortunately found at the bottom of all thinking men's minds; but made Music of' (page 232). Swinburne, not unexpectedly, took a special shine to this stanza.

23 *Kúza-Náma* is the episode of the pots. FitzGerald's dramatic sequence of connected stanzas does not reflect Khayyám's method. His order is alphabetical, determined by the last character of the rhyme word in each *rubái*. The subject and tone of each stanza range widely. In a long note FitzGerald outlines the tradition of this *'relation of Pot and Potter to Man and his Maker'*, quoting Romans ix 21: 'Hath not the potter power over the clay of the same lump to make one vessel unto honour, and another unto dishonour?'

24 We owe to the 'literalist' Graves the information that wine was actually used as a disinfectant – though he insists on a metaphorical interpretation too (that 'his friends . . . will remember only the best of him', page 25). FitzGerald's intention seems more tongue in cheek.

25 There is no garden in the original – though the idea of the garden as a focus for his 'Epicurean

eclogue' was very early in FitzGerald's mind: his summary of Khayyám's main theme to Tennyson was, 'Drink – for the Moon will often come round to look for us in this Garden and find us not.'

26 The guests mirror the sky above, and the Sáki ('Thyself' – the pourer of the wine) will mark the absence, and hold the place, of the poet – perhaps anticipating his return.